Songs from the Loom

Songs from the Loom

WE ARE STILL HERE
NATIVE AMERICANS TODAY

A Navajo Girl Learns to Weave

Text and Photographs by Monty Roessel

Lerner Publications Company ○ Minneapolis

Series Editor: Gordon Regguinti
Series Consultants: W. Roger Buffalohead, Juanita G. Corbine Espinosa

This book is available in two editions:
Library binding by Lerner Publications Company
Soft cover by First Avenue Editions
241 First Avenue North
Minneapolis, Minnesota 55401

Acknowledgments

The photographs and illustrations of Navajo rugs are used courtesy of: University of New Mexico, Maxwell Museum of Anthropology, front cover background; Ron Lynn, designer, Lula Brown, weaver/Navajo Tea & Trading Co., pp. 5, 6, 8, 12, 16, 25, 34, 40; Millicent Rogers Museum, pp. 22-23 (MRM 1956-1-11), p. 31 (MRM 1979-8), p. 33 (MRM 1956-1-1), pp. 42-43 (MRM 1956-1-6), p. 45 (MRM 1956-1-44).

The map on p. 30 is by Benson Halwood, illustrator, Ron Lynn, designer, and Lula Brown, weaver/Navajo Tea & Trading Co.

LIBRARY OF CONGRESS CATALOGING-IN-PUBLICATION DATA

Roessel, Monty.
    Songs from the loom : a Navajo girl learns to weave / Monty
Roessel.
        p.   cm. — (We are still here)
    Includes bibliographical references.
    ISBN 0–8225–2657–3 (hardcover) — ISBN 0–8225–9711–X (paperback)
    1. Navajo textile fabrics—Arizona—Kayenta—Juvenile literature.
2. Hand weaving—Arizona—Kayenta—Juvenile literature. 3. Navajo
Indians—Folklore. 4. Navajo Indians—Social life and customs—
Juvenile literature. 5. Roessel, Jaclyn. [1. Navajo textile
fabrics. 2. Hand weaving. 3. Navajo Indians—Folklore. 4. Indians
of North America—Arizona—Folklore. 5. Folklore—Arizona.
6. Navajo Indians—Social life and customs.]   I. Title.
II. Series.
E99.N3R598   1995
746.1'089'972—dc20   94-48765

Manufactured in the United States of America
1   2   3   4   5   6   –   JR   –   00   99   98   97   96   95

This book is dedicated to my parents, Bob and Ruth Roessel. Thank you for teaching your grandchildren, and me, the songs of the Navajo.

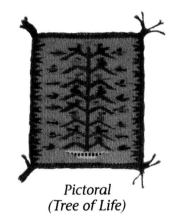

Pictoral
(Tree of Life)

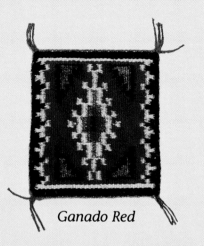

Ganado Red

Preface

Sometimes people ask me if the Navajos will be around forever. The image that jumps to mind is of my mother singing a song as she was weaving. I was seven years old at the time, and we were living away from the Navajo Reservation, in Phoenix, Arizona.

One day when I came home from school, I heard my mother's soft voice floating down the hallway from the living room. When I entered the room, she motioned me to sit by her in front of the loom. She did not stop weaving and she did not stop singing. After a few minutes, I asked why she was weaving. She told me that as long as she had her loom, she was home—in *Diné Bekayah* (Navajoland).

"This is who we are," she said. "The loom connects me with the sacred mountains, and the song connects me with my mother." She spent the next hour telling me the story of how we, the Diné—the People—learned to weave.

Recently my mind drifted back to this memory as I watched my mom tell the same stories and sing the same songs to my ten-year-old daughter, Jaclyn. This is the nature of teaching for the Navajos. One generation passes down the stories of the People to a younger generation.

While I was away at college and during difficult times, this memory of my mother singing as she wove served as a touchstone. It wasn't so much the idea of weaving that gave me strength; it was just knowing that the songs and stories were in my heart, connecting me to my home and my family. These songs affirmed who I am and made me proud of my heritage. They also made me understand the power of the stories of my people.

The main reason I became a photographer is because I grew tired of the non-Navajo world defining, through photography, who the Navajos are. I believe it is time for Navajos to tell our own stories and take our own pictures.

This book is about the way my family passes down the weaving stories of our people. I spent only a few days gathering the spoken stories, while the photographs were taken over a period of two years. Photographing the weaving process over a long period of time allowed my daughter and me to listen to the stories again and again. The more we listened, the more we learned.

A Navajo story is special. It changes a little with each telling—more details, a different perspective. That is why storytelling is so important to us. The stories define a vibrant and changing culture that is at once ancient and modern.

A friend of my daughter recently asked her why she wanted to weave. Jaclyn simply said, "That is what we do, that is who we are." Yes, there will always be Navajos, because the stories of the People live on in children like Jaclyn.

—Monty Roessel

Monty Roessel and his daughter Jaclyn

Jaclyn Roessel and her grandmother, Ruth Roessel

Burntwater

Jaclyn Roessel sat anxiously on the edge of her chair. Spread across the floor in front of her was a Navajo blanket. She stared at the intricate design of the rug as she listened to her *Nalí*—her father's mother—tell stories.

Today's story was about the Long Walk. In the 1860s, the United States Army forced 8,000 Navajos to leave their homeland in what is now called the Four Corners area of Arizona, New Mexico, Utah, and Colorado. The Navajos had to march 250 miles to Fort Sumner in eastern New Mexico. More than 3,000 people died from starvation, the cold, or bullet wounds.

But the story of the Long Walk is also one of triumph, because the *Diné* (the Navajo word for themselves, which means the People) never gave up hope that they would someday return to their homeland. After four years, their prayers were answered. The Navajos negotiated a treaty with the United States government that allowed them to go home, to *Diné Bekayah*, the land surrounded by four sacred mountains.

To the Navajos, a home is more than walls and a ceiling. A home is everything around you. The design of the traditional Navajo home, called a hogan, imitates the land. The walls are like the four mountains, and the ceiling is round, like the sky.

As Nalí Ruth ended the story, Jaclyn got off the chair and sat on the rug. She held the edge of the rug and tried to poke her finger through the yarn. She couldn't. The rug was tightly woven, a sign of a good rug.

"Nalí Ruth, can you teach me to weave?" Jaclyn said.

"*Shi Nalí,* my son's daughter, I was wondering when you were going to ask. I'll teach you, but only if you're interested in learning the Navajo way to weave," Ruth said.

Nalí Ruth joined Jaclyn on the rug. "I made this rug 40 years ago," she said as she straightened the yarns. "It looks like a simple rug, but it means so much more."

She told Jaclyn that she must know what the tools and the colors of the yarn mean and where the rug designs come from. "There is a whole world within the loom," Nalí Ruth said. "You must be willing to learn the songs and stories as well as the weaving process."

After dinner, Jaclyn and her two brothers and her baby sister got ready for bed. Their Nalí kissed them all goodnight.

As Jaclyn fell asleep, she thought about weaving. It looked like hard work, and it kind of scared her. That night she dreamed she was sitting in a hogan next to her Nalí. There were looms all around her and she went from one to another to learn. Her grandmothers and aunts teased her and she teased them. It was a lot of fun. At the end of the dream, Nalí Ruth gave Jaclyn her own small loom.

One of Jaclyn's "aunts" weaves at her loom. Navajos call any older female relative an aunt.

11

Wide Ruins

Jaclyn and her family live in Kayenta, Arizona. As reservation towns go, Kayenta is big, with more than 3,000 people. It has a Burger King, a Holiday Inn motel, a supermarket, and even a pizza place. It wasn't very long ago that Navajos had to drive many hours just to buy food at a supermarket. These days, the store is just down the street—even if some of the streets are dirt roads.

Monument Valley, with its beautiful, huge stone formations, is not far from Jaclyn's home in Kayenta.

Nalí Ruth and Bob live in Round Rock, Arizona. Even though it's also on the reservation, Round Rock is very different from Kayenta. In many ways, Round Rock looks like it did 40 years ago, when Nalí Bob arrived from St. Louis, Missouri. More than 700 people live in Round Rock, but they are hard to find. Most of them live miles from the highway. Some have homes up by the mountains, while others live on the open plateau. The town consists of a school, a trading post, and a chapter house.

The Navajo Reservation is the largest Indian reservation in the United States; it is almost the size of West Virginia. The sacred homeland extends beyond the borders of the reservation, however.

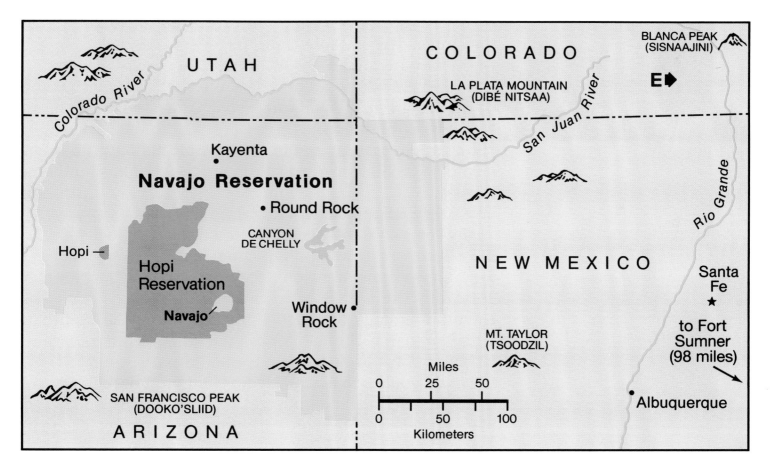

Jaclyn and her little sister, Robyn

The chapter house is the center of local government on the Navajo Reservation. There are 110 chapters throughout the Navajo Nation. If someone has a problem, they go to the chapter house to voice their concerns and seek help. Most chapters also have an elected representative who sits on the Navajo Nation Council. The Council is like a state legislature. Each chapter also elects officials to handle local issues. Nalí Ruth is the president of the Round Rock Chapter.

The Navajo Reservation is the largest Indian reservation in the United States. More than 160,000 Navajos live in the 25,000-square-mile area. Another 100,000 Navajos live in cities and towns throughout the United States. While Navajo culture is old, its people are young. More than half of all Navajos are under age 21.

Jaclyn is in the fifth grade. She attends the Kayenta Intermediate School. Like most young girls, Jaclyn has many interests outside the classroom. She likes to play basketball and volleyball and she loves in-line skating.

Fifty years ago, a ten-year-old Navajo girl like Jaclyn might have been sent to a boarding school far from home, and she would have come home only for Christmas and for summer vacation. She would have been forbidden to speak the Navajo language or practice her culture at the boarding school. A lot has changed since then. Jaclyn's mom, Karina, teaches second grade at the Kayenta Primary School. One of her main goals is to teach Navajo children that their culture has a place in the modern world. For example, Karina shows her students how their grandmothers used plants for medicine and weaving.

Jaclyn's mother, Karina, teaches Navajo culture to her second grade class.

Most schools on the reservation are required by the Navajo Nation to teach Navajo language and culture. Since there are not a lot of Navajo teachers, and almost all of the teacher's aides are Navajo, the aides usually teach these subjects.

Jaclyn was in the second grade when she first became interested in weaving. One day, her teacher's aide brought a loom into the classroom and demonstrated how to weave. She let the students try their hand at the loom. Jaclyn didn't want to stop.

Jaclyn with her grandparents, Robert and Ruth

Teec Nos Pos

The next morning when Jaclyn woke up, she knew she was ready to weave. It was still dark outside, and the sun would not rise for another hour, but Jaclyn couldn't wait. She burst into her Nalí's room and told her she wanted to weave.

Nalí Ruth and her husband, Bob, were waiting for her. They just smiled. Nalí Ruth said, "Let's get started." Jaclyn went back to her room and threw on her clothes. She followed her grandmother outside. As they left the house, Nalí Ruth reminded Jaclyn not to forget the *Tádídíín* bag she made for her, a small buckskin bag filled with corn pollen.

"Where are we going?" asked Jaclyn.

"Remember what I said last night? If you want to learn to weave, I will teach you the Navajo way. We are going to pray to the Sun and the Holy People so they will know you are learning the old ways."

They walked away from the hogan toward an open area surrounded by sagebrush and rabbit brush. Jaclyn and her Nalí stood facing the east. In the distance in front of them were the Lukachukai Mountains. The brightness from the coming sunrise threw the mountains into silhouette. But they could still see the red sandstone like a coral necklace around the bottom of the mountains.

Behind Nalí Ruth and Jaclyn were the two giant sandstone formations that give Ruth's town its name, Round Rock. In the evenings, when the sun is low on the horizon, the sandstone almost looks like it's bleeding, because the redness glows so bright.

Robert and Ruth live near Round Rock, Arizona.

Riding horseback, two Navajos herd sheep on Lukachukai Mountain.

As Jaclyn began to pray, she remembered that her grandmother had told her she should think happy thoughts as she learned to weave. Jaclyn closed her eyes and thought about the times when she helped shear sheep at her grandparents' summer sheep camp.

Many Navajos have two homes. One is for the winter and the other is for summer. During the summer, the sun dries up the grass the sheep eat, so they are herded to cooler places. People in the Round Rock community have their summer sheep camp on top of Lukachukai Mountain, where there is grass and water for the sheep and the air is cool. Every summer Jaclyn spends some time at the sheep camp.

At first when she sheared sheep, Jaclyn was afraid she would stab them. Most of the shearing was done by her grandparents. There is no electricity at the sheep camp, so the shears are manual—like big scissors. It took almost a week to shear all the sheep. Although the shearing was hard work, Jaclyn had fun chasing after the sheep and the lambs.

Nalí Ruth gave Jaclyn the *Tádídíín* bag, which was filled with corn pollen. The sun was still behind the mountain. Jaclyn put her fingers into the bag, placed some corn pollen in her mouth, then on her head, and finally sprinkled some toward the sun. As the sun came up and warmed their faces, Jaclyn and Nalí Ruth turned and walked away.

As they returned to the hogan, Nalí Ruth sang a soft song. "These are the songs of weaving," she told Jaclyn. "I learned to weave when I was four or five years old by sitting next to my mother as she wove. My mother and I would go to the trading post to sell the rugs she made. One day, I brought along a small rug that I wove. The trader thought it was nice and bought it. It was the first time I ever sold a rug. As we walked home that day, we sang a song together."

Many Navajo stories are like songs. The melodies are easy to remember. Telling a story and singing a song might be the same. Many times when grandparents talk about songs, they mean stories, because many of the prayers and songs include stories. That's how it is with the songs from the loom.

Jaclyn and Nalí Ruth sat down on the floor of the hogan. Nalí Ruth told Jaclyn the story of why the Navajos weave.

A long time ago, right after we emerged into the Fourth World—the Glittering World—there was a Holy Person named Changing Woman. She had twin boys: their names were Monster Slayer and Child Born for Water.

The twins decided to plan a secret trip. To make sure that their mother did not hear about it, the twins only discussed their plans away from the hogan. One evening while they were walking, they heard a voice. They couldn't tell where it came from. Upon hearing it the fourth time, they saw a tiny hole in the ground. They both kneeled down and looked into the hole.

All of a sudden, they were in a room with beautifully designed blankets all around them. An old woman's voice quietly said, "It is dark, my children, you shouldn't be out this late." The boys looked at her and asked her name. She told them she was Spider Woman. They told her about their secret plan, and they asked about the blankets. They had never seen anything like them before—they only knew about buckskin. They were amazed that the old Spider Woman had made them.

When they returned home, their mother asked where they had been. The boys only said they had visited an old lady who made beautiful blankets. Changing Woman was suspicious, but she became fascinated with the story of the weaver and didn't ask any more questions.

One day, Changing Woman visited Spider Woman. She wanted to see the blankets for herself. She also wanted to learn to weave. Spider Woman agreed to

teach her, with one condition. Changing Woman would have to teach other Navajo women. She agreed.

The first thing Changing Woman wanted to learn was how to make those beautiful colors and designs. Spider Woman told her the colors came from the earth. "From the east I get white, from the south I get blue, from the west I get yellow, and from the north I get black. These colors come from white shell, turquoise, abalone, and jet. But these same colors, and more, can also be made from plants.

"The designs come from the earth. Clouds, lightning, sunbeams, and mountains.

"The bottom of the loom represents the earth and the top is the sky. The strings that fasten the loom to the frame represent lightning. The warp represents the falling rain. This is why you must never weave during rain and lightning. You also must never sketch your rug before you start. The weaving must come from your mind and heart."

After Spider Woman had taught Changing Woman how to weave, she gave her one last instruction. Every rug that has a border must have an opening, a small break—usually nothing more than a light-colored piece of yarn woven into the dark border that goes to the edge of the blanket. It is sort of like an escape from the middle of the blanket. "If you don't leave an opening," she said, "you will close in your life and thoughts. You will be unable to learn any more."

Then Changing Woman went away and began to teach other women what she had learned.

Chinle

When the story was over, Nalí Ruth handed Jaclyn a paper bag. Jaclyn quickly opened it. Inside was a batten, spindle, wool carder, and other spinning and weaving tools.

"I've been waiting to give these to you," Nalí Ruth said. "Take care of them." Jaclyn kissed her Nalí and thanked her.

Then Nalí Bob brought in a small loom and set it in front of Jaclyn. "This is for you to take home so you can practice," he said. Jaclyn gave him a big hug. Excited, she asked, "What do you want me to do now?"

Nalí Ruth said it was time to card the wool. (Carding means to comb the wool so that it straightens out.) Jaclyn asked Nalí Ruth if this was the same wool they had sheared earlier in the summer. Nalí Ruth nodded her head and teased Jaclyn. "Some of the wool doesn't need to be dyed, it's already red from where you stabbed the sheep."

Jaclyn thought the wool looked like cotton candy. She was amazed that the fluffy pieces of wool that used to be on a sheep would soon be part of a rug. She carded the wool by combing it with the wool carder, a steel brush. Jaclyn brushed the wool back and forth until it was very soft and all of the tangles were gone. She then grabbed a little bit more and did the same thing over and over.

Opposite page: *Ruth shows Jaclyn how to use the wooden carder to comb wool.*

Next Jaclyn learned to spin the wool. The spindle, which looked like a small sword, lay across her lap. Holding the wool in one hand, she twisted it around the wooden spindle. When she pulled the wool away from the spindle, the strands binded together and grew and stretched into a thin string. Then she turned the spindle with her other hand until the wool wrapped around the spindle. She stretched the wool as far as she could without breaking it.

26

As her hand holding the wool came closer to the spindle, Jaclyn took another piece of wool and stretched it into a tight string. She combined the two strings and rolled them together around the spindle. As she worked, she tried not to make the wool bumpy. She remembered her Nalí telling her that it should look like hair.

The Navajo Loom

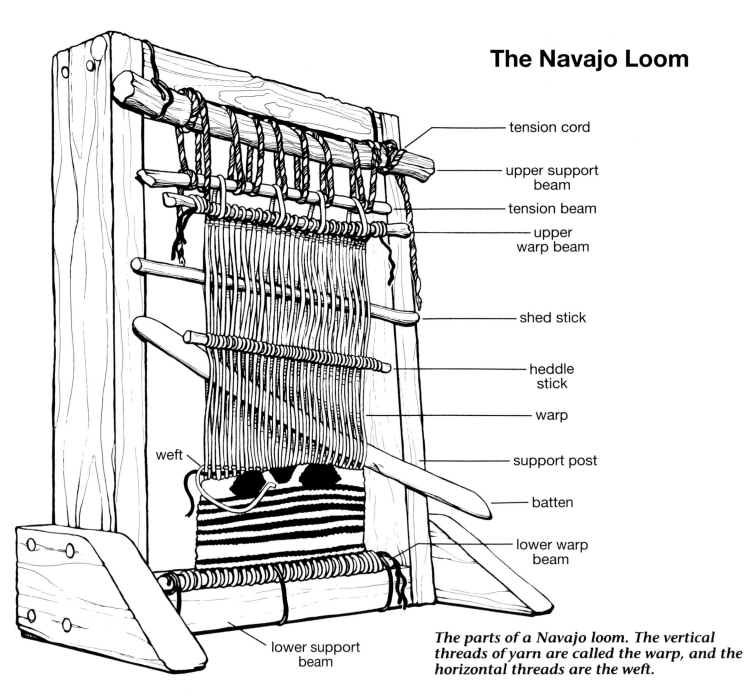

- tension cord
- upper support beam
- tension beam
- upper warp beam
- shed stick
- heddle stick
- warp
- support post
- weft
- batten
- lower warp beam
- lower support beam

The parts of a Navajo loom. The vertical threads of yarn are called the warp, and the horizontal threads are the weft.

Nalí Ruth made a frame from wood. Most Navajo people make their own looms. They look sort of like a picture frame with a stand. Then Nalí Ruth strung the loom by looping the yarn in a figure-eight pattern around the top and bottom beams. Jaclyn liked this part, because her arms were growing tired from spinning and carding the wool.

Nalí Ruth asked Jaclyn what colors she wanted to have in her rug. "You can buy whatever color you want at the arts and crafts store," Nalí Ruth said, "but you should also know how to make your own natural dyes. Yellow comes from rabbit brush. Red comes from the mountain mahogany bush. Brown and white come from brown and white sheep."

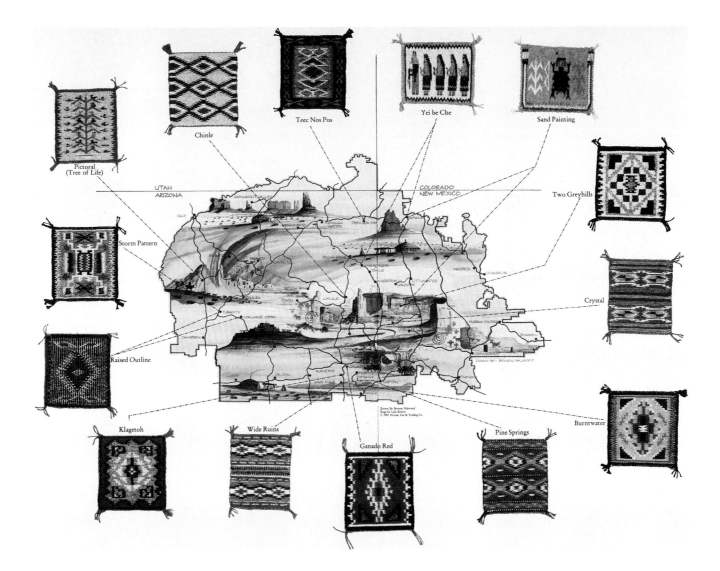

Pictoral
(Tree of Life)

Chinle

Teec Nos Pos

Yei be Che

Sand Painting

Storm Pattern

Two Greyhills

Raised Outline

Crystal

Klagetoh

Wide Ruins

Ganado Red

Pine Springs

Burntwater

Each of these rugs represents a different style of Navajo weaving.
The map shows where the various styles originated.

A Two Greyhills style rug

Navajo weavers look to the land for inspiration for the designs of their rugs. Years ago, different geographic areas were known for certain rug designs. These designs were named after the place where they were done. Ganado Red rugs, from the town of Ganado, used a rich red yarn. Coal Mine Mesa rugs were known for the raised areas on the rugs. Two Greyhills rugs were noted for their colors—white, black, and gray. These days, however, it is just as easy to find a Ganado Red rug made 150 miles away from Ganado in the town of Coal Mine Mesa, or a Coal Mine Mesa design made in Ganado.

Weaving is more than just a craft to the Navajos. It is an expression of the culture. Within the yarns of a rug is woven a rich history. Each rug is like a family story. This history is passed down from generation to generation by women.

For many Navajos, weaving is also a way to make a living. Navajo rugs hang in museums around the world. The rugs are highly valued, and weavers can sell a rug just as fast as they can make one. For some people, weaving is their only source of income.

"Today most Navajo weaving is only about money," Nalí Ruth told Jaclyn. "Some weavers don't know what the tools represent. They don't know the songs of the rug. If we forget our past, then our rugs won't mean anything. They might as well be made by a machine."

About 4 out of every 10 Navajos do not have a job, so it's understandable that some weavers only think of the money. But most Navajo weavers receive very little money for the amount of time they spend weaving. A rug that one of Jaclyn's aunts sold for $500 took one month to make. The same rug was later resold for $2,000.

The struggle to practice one's culture and still make a living is a problem facing most Indian people. Weaving is one way that some Navajos succeed in holding on to their traditions while living in a modern world.

The next morning, Jaclyn and Nalí Ruth got up early to gather plants for dyeing wool. As they walked across the dark landscape, Jaclyn stumbled over a small bush. "Nalí Ruth," Jaclyn said, "why do we always do things while it is still dark?" Her Nalí laughed and said, "The Holy People taught us that there is wisdom and beauty in the darkness before dawn. If you sleep in, you miss it."

For the next two hours they had a chance to appreciate that beauty. They walked across the flat land to a hill as the sun rose behind them. "This is what we use to make pottery," Nalí Ruth said, pointing to some clay. "But we will save that lesson for another time."

Two Greyhills

Jaclyn and Ruth drop handfuls of wool into the boiling water with the plants in it. After the wool is dyed, it is removed with a stick from the boiling water. Later, when the dyed wool is dry, Jaclyn removes pieces of plants that are stuck in it.

When they got back home, Jaclyn helped as Nalí Ruth prepared to dye the wool. A big fire was built and pots of water were placed on a grill over the flames. When the water came to a boil, Nalí Ruth dropped the plants into the pots. After the plants boiled for about 30 minutes, some of the unspun wool was put into the pots. The longer the wool boiled in the vegetable dye, the richer the color became. It was sort of like coloring Easter eggs, Jaclyn thought. After about an hour, they removed the wool with a stick and laid it out to dry on the rocks next to the fire.

Jaclyn and Ruth make some fry bread while the fire is still hot. They drop the batter into hot oil and it puffs up into a crisp, golden, round piece of fry bread.

While the wool dried, Jaclyn went back to the loom. Her grandmother had started a rug on it already. Jaclyn threaded a piece of red yarn horizontally through the vertical strings. Using the comb, she blended the new yarn into the rug that her grandmother had already started by pushing it close to the other yarns. She then threaded a black piece through the strings and firmly combed it into the existing pattern. She followed the design that Nalí Ruth was already weaving.

After a couple of hours, Jaclyn became frustrated—her lines were crooked. She felt like she would never learn. She was afraid she had ruined her Nalí's rug forever. Nalí Ruth just laughed.

39

Jaclyn and her brothers Bryan and Robert are sad to leave their grandparents' home.

Yei Be Che

At the end of the week, Jaclyn had to return home to Kayenta. She wanted to remember everything her Nalí had told her, but it was impossible. There was just too much information, too many steps, and too many stories. As Jaclyn got into the car with her parents and brothers, Nalí Ruth said, "Don't worry about remembering everything. It is inside you now. You will remember what to do when you have to."

The 75-mile drive back to Kayenta took a little more than an hour. It was more than enough time for Jaclyn to decide where to put the loom her grandparents had given her. Jaclyn hurried into the house with the loom clutched tightly in both hands. She went directly to her room and set the loom on top of her desk, next to her homework.

Every day after school Jaclyn spent some time working on her weaving. Some days it was only 15 minutes, and other days she spent hours. It was like homework—something she had to do but also something she wanted to do.

The next month, Nalí Ruth surprised Jaclyn with a visit. She wanted to see how Jaclyn's weaving was coming along. When she walked into Jaclyn's room, she saw the weaving tools lying all over the room. She sat down next to Jaclyn and asked why she wasn't taking care of her tools. Jaclyn felt like she had let her Nalí down. Nalí Ruth put her arms around her and said, "Let me tell you a story."

After school Jaclyn works on her weaving at her desk at home.

One day a young lady came to Changing Woman and said she wanted to learn to weave. Changing Woman taught her, just like I have taught you. After spending days and days in front of the loom, the woman had made no progress on the rug. She didn't understand why nothing was happening. The lady was so tired that she fell asleep in front of the loom. Finally, on the fourth day she got so mad she tore the loom down and threw all her weaving tools away. She threw the comb in one direction, the batten in another. She never wanted to see them again.

Four days later, she thought she heard a baby crying. She looked out her doorway but saw nothing. Again she heard the cry. This time she went to investigate. When she reached the spot she thought the crying had come from, she looked closely at the ground. In front of her, underneath a sagebrush, was her weaving comb. The comb was crying. She heard another cry from a different direction. When she got closer she saw her batten lying on a yucca plant. The batten too was crying.

She held the tools in her hand and looked at them. She couldn't believe what was happening. The comb looked at the woman and told her, "I am crying because you threw me away. You didn't appreciate me and the other tools—that is why your rug never grew while you were weaving. You must never sleep on the ground in front of a loom because that is disrespectful."

The young woman felt guilty. She had betrayed not only her tools but her people. The woman gathered all of her tools and made a special buckskin bag that became their home. Over time, she made many beautiful blankets and was able to clothe herself and her family.

Remember this story when you are weaving. Always take care of your tools and they will take care of you.

Nalí Ruth and Jaclyn sat quietly before the small loom. Now that Jaclyn knew the stories and the steps of weaving, there was only one thing left. "It is time to learn the songs of weaving," Nalí Ruth said.

Very slowly at first, Nalí Ruth recited the Navajo words, like a poem. Gradually it became a song.

I weave in harmony.
With the Earth I weave.
The strings are like rain,
The rain touches my fingers.
There is beauty in my rug.
There is beauty all around me.
The plants speak to me,
Mother Earth colors my rug.
I weave in harmony.

Together they worked on the rug. Together they sang a song. The stories were told, the techniques taught and learned, and now the songs were sung. It was time to weave.

Word List

batten—a piece of wood used to hold the yarn in place on a loom

card—to comb wool so that the curls straighten out

Diné *(dee-NEH)*—Navajo word meaning "the People," which Navajos use to describe themselves

Diné Bekayah *(dee-NEH be-KAY-ah)*—the Navajo homeland, which lies between four sacred mountains (Sisnaajini, Tsoodzil, DookO'Sliid, and Dibé Nitsaa) in the Four Corners area of Arizona, Utah, Colorado, and New Mexico

hogan *(ho-GAHN)*—an eight-sided structure that is the traditional Navajo home

Holy People—Navajo spiritual beings

Nalí *(nuh-LEH)*—father's mother or father

reservation—an area of land that Indian people kept through agreement with the United States government

Shi Nalí *(shih-nuh-LEH)*—son's daughter or son

spin—to stretch and pull wool into strings of yarn

spindle—a round stick used to hold and turn wool as it is spun

Tádídíín *(tah-da-deen)*—a small buckskin bag filled with corn pollen

warp—the vertical threads of yarn on a loom

weft—the horizontal threads of yarn on a loom

For Further Reading

Berlant, Anthony, and Mary Hunt Kahlenberg. *Walk in Beauty: The Navajo and Their Blankets.* Boston: New York Graphic Society, 1977.

Between Sacred Mountains: Navajo Stories and Lessons from the Land. Vol. II, SUN TRACKS. Tucson, AZ: Sun Tracks and the University of Arizona Press, 1982.

Dockstader, Frederick J. *The Song of the Loom: New Traditions in Navajo Weaving.* New York: Hudson Hills Press in association with the Montpelier Art Museum, 1987.

Iverson, Peter. *The Navajos.* New York: Chelsea House Pub., 1990.

Kaufman, Alice, and Christopher Selser. *The Navajo Weaving Tradition: 1650 to the Present.* New York: Dutton, 1985.

Roessel, Robert A. *Navajo Arts and Crafts.* Rough Rock, AZ: Rough Rock Demonstration School, Navajo Curriculum Center, 1983.

Roessel, Ruth, ed. *Stories of Traditional Navajo Life and Culture.* Tsaile, AZ: Navajo Community College Press, 1977.

About the Author

Monty Roessel is a photographer and writer who specializes in contemporary Native Americans, especially the Navajos. Upon graduation from the University of Northern Colorado, he worked for various newspapers as a photographer and editor before becoming a freelance photojournalist. His photographs have appeared in many magazines, including *Time, Newsweek, Arizona Highways, The New York Times Magazine,* and *Sports Illustrated.* Roessel's work also appears in books such as *Baseball in America, Photographing Arizona, Native America,* and *Circle of Nations.* He is the author of *Kinaaldá: A Navajo Girl Grows Up.* When not on assignment, Roessel works on a personal project documenting, from a Navajo's perspective, contemporary Navajo life.

Series Contributors

Series Editor **Gordon Regguinti** is a member of the Leech Lake Band of Ojibway. He was raised on Leech Lake Reservation by his mother and grandparents. His Ojibway heritage has remained a central focus of his professional life. A graduate of the University of Minnesota with a B.A. in Indian Studies, Regguinti has written about Native American issues for newspapers and school curricula. He served as editor of the Twin Cities native newspaper *The Circle* for two years and as executive director of the National Association of Native American Journalists. He lives in Minneapolis and has six children and one grandchild.

Series Consultant **W. Roger Buffalohead**, Ponca, has been involved in Indian Education for more than 20 years, serving as a national consultant on issues of Indian curricula and tribal development. He has a B.A. in American History from Oklahoma State University and an M.A. from the University of Wisconsin, Madison. Buffalohead has taught at the University of Cincinnati, the University of California, Los Angeles, and the University of Minnesota, where he was director of the American Indian Learning and Resources Center. Currently he teaches at the American Indian Arts Institute in Santa Fe, New Mexico. Among his many activities, Buffalohead is a founding board member of the National Indian Education Association and a member of the Cultural Concerns Committee of the National Conference of American Indians. He lives in Santa Fe.

Series Consultant **Juanita G. Corbine Espinosa**, Dakota/Ojibway, is the director of Native Arts Circle, Minnesota's first statewide Native American arts agency. She is first and foremost a community organizer, active in a broad range of issues, many of which are related to the importance of art in community life. In addition, she is a board member of the Minneapolis American Indian Center and an advisory member of the Minnesota State Arts Board's Cultural Pluralism Task Force.